Growing Up Daisy

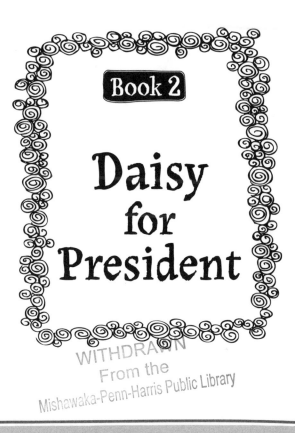

Book 2

Daisy
for
President

By: Marci Peschke
Illustrated by: M.H. Pilz

Mishawaka-Penn-Harris
Public Library
Mishawaka, Indiana

visit us at www.abdopublishing.com

To Para Mis Amigas: Joy, Gay & Parna - MP
For Matthew - MHP

 This book contains at least 10% recycled materials.

Text by Marci Peschke
Illustrated by M.H. Pilz
Edited by Stephanie Hedlund and Rochelle Baltzer
Cover and interior design by Abbey Fitzgerald

Library of Congress Cataloging-in-Publication Data

Peschke, M. (Marci)
  Daisy for president / by Marci Peschke ; illustrated by M.H. Pilz.
     p. cm. -- (Growing up Daisy ; bk. 2)
  ISBN 978-1-61641-115-2 (alk. paper)
  1. Pilz, MH, ill. II. Title.
  PZ7.P441245Dai 2011
  [Fic]--dc22

                              2010028455

Table of Contents

1
No Contest

Daisy Martinez and her best friend Blanca were listening to the morning announcements. Mrs. Miller, the school counselor, announced that the student council elections would be held in two weeks.

She added that students who wished to run for office should see her for a form and rules for campaigning. Then she asked them to stand for the Pledge of Allegiance. Chairs scratched the tile floor as the students from room 210 rose to face the American flag.

Daisy was excited to be ten years old in room 210. She was sure it was a sign she'd have a good year in fourth grade. So far, the year had been great. Daisy was in the same class as her BFF and they had the cool new teacher Ms. Lilly.

Daisy whispered to Blanca, "Who do you think will run for president?" She put her hand over heart and began to say the pledge, but she was looking at Blanca.

Blanca started to say the pledge too, "I pledge allegiance to Jason and to the fourth grade class," she said giggling. No one but Daisy heard her.

After they finished the last few words, they both sat down. Daisy agreed, "Jason would be a great president. He is super smart and hardworking. Let's ask him at lunch to run for fourth grade president."

Ms. Lilly was standing at the front of the room with her sparkly red glasses sitting on the end of her nose. She called, "Attention, my superstar students, attention! We have some very important business to discuss. Mrs. Miller has asked that every class have a boy and a girl class representative for the Townsend Elementary student council."

No one was in a hurry to raise a hand, so Ms. Lilly asked if anyone would volunteer. Still not a single student was willing to stay after school and be a voting member of the student council for the class.

Ms. Lilly stood in the front of the room looking astonished. She cried, "Not a single one of you wants to have this special honor?"

Finally Jason raised his hand and said, "Okay, I'll do it. But only because I know our council should be ruled by the students and for the students."

Their teacher happily wrote his name on the slip of paper the counselor put in her box. She gave Jason two thumbs-up and proceeded with her quest to find a girl volunteer. Before long Amber agreed to be the second representative for room 210.

Daisy and Blanca both looked at each other. Now Jason would not be running for president since he had already decided to be a class representative. Daisy wondered who would be running for president.

Maybe a kid from another fourth grade class, she thought. *It could be someone from Min or DeShaye's classes.*

While Daisy was considering the possibilities, Madison raised her hand and waved it back and forth excitedly. She didn't even wait to be called on. Instead, she jumped up and blurted out, "I'm running for president!"

Her best friend Lizzie started clapping and chanting *"Madison, Madison, Madison."* Blanca blinked in surprise. Daisy was not as surprised, since Madison liked being the center of attention.

"I sure hope someone runs against her," Blanca said. "A little power in her hands could be a really bad thing."

Daisy always tried to see the best in everyone. She carefully suggested, "Maybe she would be a good president, since she likes to be in charge of things."

Behind her Raymond grunted, "I don't think so . . ." Then he banged his head on his desk twice as if the idea of Madison in charge was torturing him.

"She has wanted to be the boss since we were in first grade," Blanca said.

Raymond just shook his head saying, "I don't think I want her to be the president."

It seemed to Daisy that the whole thing was out of their hands anyway. Ms. Lilly had already sent Madison to get the forms.

Blanca blurted out, "We're doomed!"

Daisy feared that her friend might be right, but she preferred to stay positive. After all, another candidate could run against Madison, right?

Daisy twisted the end of her charcoal black braid. Ms. Lilly wrote D.E.A.R. on the board. That meant *Drop Everything And Read*. Daisy would have to at least pretend to read her book while considering who could run against Madison.

While she pretended, Daisy wished she could make a list. Lists were one of her favorite things to write. Every day she made lists for homework, things to do, *amigas* to call, and stuff she needed to remember.

In her head, Daisy began a list without writing it down. She thought that Sophie or Lizzie might be good leaders since they were nice and earned good grades. Camden was cool. Kenzie was too. Eric was too sporty.

What about Mr. Harrison's class, Daisy thought. DeShaye for president . . . maybe not. Even though they were good friends, Daisy was not sure that the way DeShaye said whatever was on her mind, nice or not, would help her win an election.

Out of the corner of her eye, Daisy saw a swish of hot pink lace. Ms. Lilly's skirt was right beside her desk and that meant Ms. Lilly was, too!

Daisy had been so distracted making a mental list that she accidently closed her book and laid it on her desk.

Ms. Lilly crouched down beside Daisy's desk. She whispered, "Unless you have special powers, Daisy, it would be impossible to read your book when it is closed on your desk. Is everything okay?"

Daisy's eyes darted around the room. The kids in room 210 were all reading except her and Madison, who burst into the room at that precise moment and boldly announced she had no competition.

Ms. Lilly stood up. Raymond asked, "Do we still get to vote if no one runs against Madison?"

Looking a little bit unsure, their teacher explained that, being new to their school, she was not familiar with the student council rules. But, she continued that in her mind no opponent meant no contest.

"Great," moaned Raymond.

Blanca leaned over and said, "I told you we're doomed!"

2

The Presidential Pain

At lunch a few hours later, the talk at Daisy's table was all about the student council elections.

Blanca and Daisy always sat with their friends Min and DeShaye. Mami said that Min always talked like a grown-up. DeShaye was a really good tennis player. She even had a coach and went to competitions.

DeShaye said, "You know, I could rule this school, but I don't need the drama."

"What if Madison is the only candidate?" Min worried. Between bites they all imagined the things she might do as president.

"I bet she makes new rules," Blanca declared. "Like assigning seats at lunch."

This made Raymond freak out. He asked, "Can she make rules as president?"

Daisy assured everyone that the power of the class president was limited. She told them that only the principal could be the "real" boss of the school.

Daisy could tell Raymond was thinking about that at his end of the table.

Today, Min was eating egg rolls. Daisy had little burritos for her lunch and they looked a lot like Min's egg rolls. She held one up for Min to see. Min held up an egg roll and they both laughed. They were lunch buddies. Nearly every day they brought almost the same thing for lunch.

The discussion swung back around to the upcoming elections. Raymond leaned closer so he could hear better. It was very noisy in the cafeteria. Kids were banging trays and talking to each other.

If it got too loud the lunch monitor, Mrs. Claudia, would hold up her hand as a signal that they were too loud. After the third warning, they would not be able to talk for the rest of the lunch period.

On the other side of the room, Madison was talking about being president. She said in a very loud voice, "I will be the best president ever."

Everyone heard her. She was so loud that Mrs. Claudia raised her hand. It was their second warning. Some kids at the table next to Madison's tried to shush her.

Madison kept going on and on. She was getting her friends all excited by promising to have lip gloss in the girls' bathroom when she was president.

Min said, "Eeew, I think that is a terrible idea. We would all be passing our germs around. I would never wear it, because I wouldn't like being sick and missing school."

Min had perfect attendance. In fact, she had not missed a day since kindergarten.

Daisy added, "My parents don't allow me to wear lip gloss anyway." From the other side of the room they heard Madison's BFFs chanting, "Madison, Madison, Madison."

They all looked over just in time to see the third warning. Now, no one could make a peep until lunch was over in ten minutes.

Kids all over the cafeteria were glaring at Madison. When they finally got up to go out for recess, DeShaye was super mad. It was really difficult for her to keep quiet. Talking was like breathing to DeShaye.

Outside the sun was warm on their backs, so Daisy, Min, Blanca, and DeShaye just sat on the grass talking. Blanca had a cootie catcher. She kept saying, "Pick a number. Pick a color." Then after she opened and closed it, she would unfold it and read what it said.

Inside it said things like *you're cool, you'll get an A on your test, you will make a new friend,* and so on. DeShaye got *you're cool* when she played. She bragged, "You know it!"

Madison and her crowd were all sitting on the benches and at the picnic table by the building. They would never sit on the grass,

because that would *not* be cool. Besides, they might get a little dirty.

Daisy thought sitting on the grass was fun. *If you're too cool you probably miss out on a lot of fun stuff,* she decided.

Daisy saw Raymond making and throwing paper airplanes on the other side of the monkey bars. Making cootie catchers and paper planes was fun. Daisy was glad she was not too cool for fun!

After recess, they returned to room 210. Ms. Lilly began class by pointing to a giant map of the world. She started talking about England and King James. Then she told the class that they would be studying the pilgrims.

That explains a lot of things! Daisy thought. When they came back in from recess, she had noticed that Ms. Lilly had braided her hair. A long grey and back feather was sticking out of the braid. Ms. Lilly was a very surprising teacher. None of the kids ever knew what she might do next!

Ms. Lilly announced that each student would be given a person to research. She began to pass out slips to the students.

Daisy almost clapped when she saw that she got Pocahontas. Blanca got a pilgrim wife. Raymond got a pilgrim child.

Madison was telling Lizzie that she wanted to be King James, but Jason ended up being the king. Madison ended up getting William Bradford.

Raymond muttered, "If she got to be king she would be a royal pain."

Blanca passed Daisy a note that said, "A presidential pain is more like it!" Daisy slipped the note under her social studies folder.

Next, the class read a story about the Puritans. They were the first settlers in a colony called Jamestown. It was named after the king of England.

One thing was certain, pilgrims did not have much fun. They worked a lot! Hearing about their struggles made Daisy tired. It was almost three o'clock and time for the bell to ring. She couldn't wait to go home and see what *Abuela* made for their after school snack.

Ring ring the afternoon bell sounded. Blanca began to stuff her notebook in her backpack. She said, "Call me tonight and we can talk about the presidential pain."

Daisy nodded, but she didn't know what difference talking about it would make.

When she got home the whole house smelled like cookies. Abuela had cookies and milk waiting for their snack. Her brothers were already sitting at the table.

When Manuel saw Daisy, he pulled the plate of cookies in front of him. "All mine!" he warned her.

Abuela scowled, adding, "*¡Mi jos*, you have to share!" Daisy just ignored them. It would be better to stand in the kitchen with Abuela and have cookies right out of the oven.

The snack was so tasty, Daisy licked the chocolate off her fingers and gulped down some icy milk. Then she helped finish baking the cookies.

Later that night, just before bedtime, she called Blanca. Her friend only wanted to talk about Madison. She didn't want to make a plan to find someone else who would be a good president.

Finally, Mami told Daisy it was time to hang up and get ready for bed. Daisy said good-bye to Blanca and hung up the phone.

When Daisy went upstairs, she found Paola was already tucked in for the night. Daisy tried to be extra quiet putting on her nightgown. She could hear her *hermana* snoring and Abuela breathing. It was hard to go to sleep with three people in a room sometimes, but it was cozy, too.

3
Daisy Power

The next day, Daisy was sleepy. It was hard to wake up when Mami called her to get ready for school. It had taken her long time to fall asleep the night before. Daisy had been wondering if they should try to get DeShaye to change her mind and run for president after all.

Now it was time to get ready for school. First, she got dressed because her brothers were brushing their teeth in the bathroom. When they finished, she rushed in before anyone else could beat her to it.

Looking in the mirror, Daisy saw that she still had gunk in eyes from sleeping. She washed her face and brushed her hair.

Daisy took one last look in the mirror thinking that she looked nice. She had on a crisp white blouse and her khaki jumper. In her room she added a gold bracelet, some rainbow-colored bangles, and earrings that looked like peace signs. No longer tired, she headed downstairs for breakfast.

"Eat fast, *mi ja*," Abuela said, "or you will be late for school." Daisy wrapped a sausage in a pancake and headed for the front door. Her siblings were already at the corner.

Running with breakfast in one hand and lunch in the other was tricky. At anytime she could trip or step in a crack in the sidewalk.

It seemed like Manuel and Diego were speeding up because she never seemed to catch them. Paola was skipping beside them.

Finally, Daisy gave up. She decided it would be better to walk alone and eat her breakfast before she got to school. So she did.

Daisy was standing by the flagpole in front of the school when she heard the tardy bell ring. Oh no! She was late. This meant she would have to get a tardy slip from the office before she could go to class.

Speeding up, Daisy sprinted into the office just in time to hear Ms. Miller announce that Wednesday was the last day to sign up to run for student council.

As the door closed behind Daisy, the clerk asked her why she was late. Daisy paused. She didn't know whether to say eating breakfast made her late or that she took too long in the bathroom. Both sounded bad, so she settled for saying that she hadn't been ready for school in time.

With the pink tardy slip in her hand, she hurried to her classroom. She hated being late. It was embarrassing.

She pushed open the door and eighteen pairs of eyes blinked in her direction.

Ms. Lilly asked, "Daisy, do you have a tardy slip?"

Daisy presented the pink paper to her teacher. Ms. Lilly thanked her and asked her to take her seat. Blanca could hardly wait for her to sit down before she passed a note asking why she was late.

Daisy scribbled an answer then passed it back across the aisle. Blanca's mouth made a perfect O and she nodded her head.

Ms. Lilly began the day by reading aloud from a pilgrim journal. They sure talked funny back then. Who knew Old English could sound so different than English? They said *Ye* a lot and not like *yee haw*.

The morning crawled along until finally they could go to lunch. Daisy decided that school was harder when you were sleepy.

At lunch DeShaye, Min, and Blanca didn't even bring up the student council elections. Madison was busy talking about William Bradford at her table. They could hear her bragging that she was the boss of the settlement.

After eating her sandwich, Daisy's energy level picked up. When it was time to go out for recess, Daisy and her friends sat on the grass again. Blanca pulled out her cootie catcher.

Min usually liked to play, but she said, "Daisy, you play first." Blanca opened and closed it a few times then said, "Pick a number." Daisy picked three.

After opening and closing the cootie catcher three times, Blanca said, "Pick a color." Daisy picked red since it was Ms. Lilly's favorite color. Blanca started to giggle.

She said, "You will run for class president." Daisy shrieked, "No way! Gimme that." She grabbed the cootie catcher and opened it. She saw that no matter what color or number she picked they all said, *You will run for class president.*

Leaning back she looked at her BFFs. She asked, "When did you decide I should be the president?"

DeShaye replied, "Girl, we talked about it and decided you were perfect for the job."

Min's short black hair bobbed up and down as she agreed. Daisy was a little surprised.

"Really? Me?" she asked.

Blanca explained, "You are nice and smart, so kids will want to vote for you instead of Madison. Min is too shy. I will be too busy being your campaign manager to run, and DeShaye already said no."

Daisy was having a hard time deciding if it was a crazy idea or a good one.

Min begged, "Please, Daisy! You would be so good. Kids in my class already want to vote for you. I told them you might run."

There wasn't any more time to discuss it because it started to rain and they all had to run inside. Recess was almost over anyway.

The afternoon went by pretty quick since they were only doing a review for the next day's math test. Daisy was not a great math student, so she wished the cootie catcher had said *You will get an* A *on your next test.* She might anyway. It was just going to be multiplication and a few word problems.

Blanca had been doodling all through the review and she finally handed Daisy a paper. It had a lot of slogans on it.

Daisy for President.
Daisy Rocks.
Daisy Power.

Blanca had sketched a bunch of daisies along the edge of the paper. Then, she had drawn an arrow over to Daisy Power.

At the bottom she wrote, "I like Daisy Power. Write down some words that describe the characteristics you have that would make you a good class president."

Daisy wrote back, "I didn't say I would do it yet."

Behind her Raymond groaned, "Do it, Daisy, or we'll get Madison for sure!" He must have been reading her note over her shoulder.

Blanca whispered, "Who asked you?"

Raymond muttered, "No one." Then, he put his head on his desk. Daisy knew she could be a good president. She liked everyone and was fair.

The big question was, would kids vote for her? Daisy Power sounded cute. She reached for Blanca's paper and wrote on the bottom *fair, nice, creative, caring,* and *smart.*

Then she added, *You can be my manager. We make a great team!*

Daisy passed the note back to Blanca. As soon as Blanca read it, she raised her hand.

Ms. Lilly asked, "What is it, Blanca?"

Blanca shouted, "Daisy is running for class president!"

Everyone started clapping. Ms. Lilly said, "Yay for democracy! Good luck to both superstar students, Madison and Daisy."

Madison turned around in her seat to face Daisy. She shouted, "You are just a copycat, Daisy Martinez!" Then she crossed her arms and pouted for the rest of the day.

The bell rang about thirty minutes later. Daisy and Blanca practically ran out of room 210 to find DeShaye and Min. They couldn't wait to tell them that they were ready to begin the campaign. They were going to spread the message of Daisy Power all over the school!

4

Happy Headquarters

That night, Daisy could hardly wait to tell her family about her decision to run for president. But she wanted to tell them all at once, so she waited until dinnertime.

Everyone sat down once the table was loaded with food. Papi had grilled chicken and Abuela made rice, beans, and homemade tortillas. Yummy!

As the family began to pass the food around the table Daisy said, "I have some exciting news!"

Manuel said, "Let me guess, you're moving to Mars!"

Diego gave him a high five saying, "Good one, *hermano*!"

Daisy just ignored her brothers. Soon their mouths would be too full to talk. She repeated Mrs. Miller's announcement and told them all that Madison was running for president.

"That's good, mi ja," Abuela said. "Are you going to help this girl?"

Daisy took a deep breath. Smiling, she admitted, "No, I am also going to run for president."

All around the table, silverware clinked on plates as everyone stopped eating. Usually the table was noisy, but suddenly it was silent.

Abuela stammered, "Daisy *para presidenta*?"

Mami jumped in, "What a wonderful challenge!"

Daisy was waiting for Papi to approve. He bragged, "You will win! I know it." Then, the entire family started to eat again.

Then Paola said, "I can't wait to vote for you, Daisy."

Manuel looked at Diego and asked, "Are you voting for her?"

Before he could say anything Papi said, "Voting is a private matter. You should think carefully about who will do the best job. I would vote for Daisy because she will be a good president."

Both boys carefully considered the options. Diego finally said, "Madison is mean. I'm voting for Daisy, Manuel. You make up your own mind."

Manuel did not say who he would vote for. That night after dinner, the phone kept ringing and ringing.

Mami finally got tired of answering the phone and told Daisy to stay near it. Some kids that Daisy didn't even know called to say congratulations.

Min called last. She reminded Daisy that she had to see Mrs. Miller for the paperwork required to be in the presidential race.

Once again, Daisy had trouble sleeping. But she wasn't worried this time, just excited.

Papi dropped Daisy off at school the next morning. She wanted to be super early to see Mrs. Miller. That way she could have everything completed before the first bell rang.

The counselor was always at school early. When Daisy knocked on the door Mrs. Miller said, "Come in. Can I help you, Daisy?"

Daisy told her she had decided to run for student council president. She asked Mrs. Miller for the paperwork.

"Daisy, you rock!" Mrs. Miller said as she handed Daisy the paperwork. "I think it is great that we'll have a real contest for student council president."

Right away, Daisy sat down at the table on the far end of the office. She used her lucky purple pen to fill everything out, except the place that asked for a parent's signature.

Daisy showed Mrs. Miller the completed paper. Since her mami worked at the school part-time, Mrs. Miller offered to get her to sign it when she came in.

Daisy thanked Mrs. Miller and headed for class. The first bell rang as she was on her way, but her BFFs were waiting by her locker.

"Did you get it done?" Blanca asked.

Daisy nodded, "Yes, now we can get started."

"I think we better get on it," DeShaye said. "Madison has already started to put up posters." She pointed to one over the water fountain. It was white with red letters and blue sparkly stars on it. It read *VOTE Madison for Superstar President*.

Daisy blurted out, "She copied that from our teacher! Ms. Lilly says *superstar* all the time. Right, Blanca?"

Blanca's face was red. She was really mad. Daisy assured her, "Don't worry. Your idea for me is more fun."

Min added, "I like Daisy Power better."

Blanca was going to say something when the warning bell sounded. They all dashed toward their classrooms.

DeShaye said over her shoulder, "We'll talk at lunch."

Once in room 210, Daisy and Blanca slumped in their chairs out of breath. Ms. Lilly said, "Good morning, superstar students! You will have all morning to work on your social studies assignment."

Then, Ms. Lilly called Madison and Daisy to the front of the room. She explained that every good campaign needed someplace to work. So, she had arranged for Madison to use an empty janitor's closet and Daisy to use a tiny testing room.

Immediately Madison complained about getting the closet. Daisy offered, "Madison, you can have the testing room if you want. It's okay with me."

Madison insisted, "Good. I need the real room for my headquarters, because I am going to win and you are going to lose."

Ms. Lilly reminded her that *thank you* was the polite thing to say to Daisy. Madison grudgingly thanked Daisy. Then they both returned to their seats.

Blanca quietly asked, "What was that about?"

Daisy whispered, "I am so excited! Ms. Lilly is giving us a place to set up campaign headquarters." Blanca and Daisy continued working on their assignment and passing notes until lunchtime.

At lunch, Blanca told everyone about her plans. They would use their recess time to check out the closet.

"Let's hurry and eat," DeShaye suggested. "Then we can ask Mrs. Claudia to let us go early." Everyone agreed. No one was talking, instead everyone was eating.

In ten minutes they were done. Min raised her hand and Mrs. Claudia came over.

"Do you need the girls' bathroom pass?" she asked.

Min shook her head no. She explained where they were going and politely asked if they could please be excused. Mrs. Claudia asked some questions and gave them a note. As they stood up to go, Raymond stood up, too.

Blanca asked, "Where are you going?"

Raymond didn't answer and just sat back down. Daisy guessed he wanted to come, too. She said, "Come on, Raymond. I need all the help I can get to win."

Two hallways and twelve doors later, they were standing in front of the janitor's closet. When they opened the door, the faint scent of pine trees filled the air.

Inside there were shelves all along one wall and a small desk in the middle. A stack of brightly colored plastic chairs sat in one corner. For a closet, it was a pretty large space. They could probably fit five more kids in and not be squished.

They all decided they would bring some stuff to make it look less like a closet. Min was going to bring a lamp with flowers on the shade. DeShaye was going to bring a beaded curtain for the doorway. Blanca said she had some colorful plastic baskets from her bedroom to put things on the shelves.

Blanca wrote everything down in a spiral notebook with a huge flower on the front. In the center of the flower she had written in black marker: Daisy Power.

Next, she outlined their strategy. They would need posters, stickers, and other ideas to get the word out. In less than two short weeks the school would be voting.

Daisy looked at all of her friends and gave a small speech. She began, "I would like to win, but this is about doing our best. Win or lose, I'll still have all of you and having you for friends makes me happy."

They gathered in a circle and all put their hands in the center. When all the hands were in Daisy said, "To having a fun adventure!"

Then Min added, "To our happy headquarters!"

5

Campaign Chaos

The next day was so busy it was crazy! Daisy wanted to get to school early to put the poster supplies Mami helped her buy in her new headquarters. Papi drove her to school because she had so many bags to carry.

On her way to her headquarters, she passed Madison's headquarters. Daisy couldn't believe her eyes! Madison must have stayed *very* late the night before. Her door was covered with 100 red stars. A campaign poster with a huge photo of Madison was in the middle.

Daisy had to admit, the photo was a great idea. Maybe she could use it in another way. It wouldn't be nice to totally copy Madison.

After she got everything organized, Daisy started to make posters. They were giant daisies and in the middle they said, "Daisy Power!" On each of the centers she wrote a word like *fair, nice, creative,* or *smart.* Two posters were finished by the time Blanca got to school.

Daisy said, "I'm so glad you're here! I was getting bored making these all by myself. How do you like them?"

Blanca put down her backpack and looked at the orange and lime green daisy posters.

She exclaimed, "Oooh, too cute! I can't wait to make some."

Daisy made room for Blanca to work. Blanca said, "We only have about thirty minutes before the first bell. I bet I can get a few posters done by then." She added, "Did you see Madison's door?"

Daisy groaned, "It would be hard to miss!" They both worked and talked about campaign ideas. Daisy told Blanca that she might want to use her picture on stickers to pass out on voting day.

DeShaye and Min joined them in time to hear her plan. DeShaye commented, "Sounds cool to me."

Min was busy looking at the posters. She held one up to admire it. "These are beautiful!" she said with excitement.

Since they didn't have enough room for everyone to make posters, DeShaye and Min took some to hang up in the fourth grade hall.

By the time the bell rang they had eight posters finished and all of them were already hung up.

When Daisy and Blanca got to room 210, Ms. Lilly was getting everything ready for them to watch a DVD about pilgrim life. Daisy was glad. That meant she wouldn't have social studies homework. Maybe Blanca could come over to her house and they could get the stickers made.

When Ms. Lilly turned out the lights and started the DVD, Raymond put his head on his desk. Before long, Daisy heard him snoring. She tried to poke him with the eraser of her pencil. He just grunted and moved his head to the other side of the desk.

Daisy nudged him with her elbow. Raymond moved his head so far that it fell off the desk, causing him to lose his balance. He was lucky he didn't tip over the desk.

"Why did you wake me up?" Raymond muttered. Daisy turned a little in her chair and whispered, "We're in school, remember?"

Raymond didn't comment, but at least he was awake now. The morning passed quickly, especially when Ms. Lilly let both Daisy and Blanca go work on the campaign after they finished their math assignment.

When they got to headquarters, Daisy and Blanca decided the door of their headquarters definitely needed something to jazz it up.

They had already put the lamp Min brought on the desk. The baskets from Blanca were on the shelves filled with markers, scissors, and tape. Now, they added DeShaye's beaded curtain to the doorway. These small things made a huge difference in the dull closet. It was kind of cheerful now.

Blanca suggested, "I think you should make some campaign announcements after the pledge in the morning."

Daisy thought that was a fantastic idea. The announcements would have to be short. Min was an excellent writer and would be a good person to ask to write them. Daisy decided she would ask her at lunch.

Raymond called, "Hey!" Daisy and Blanca were surprised that he showed up.

"Don't you have work to do?" Blanca asked. Raymond explained that he was already finished. Blanca, who was feeling very important as campaign manager, sent him to the computer lab to check out a camera.

Blanca explained that they needed to get a picture of Daisy soon. They only had seven more days until voting, so there was no time to waste. Besides Daisy's hot pink socks and the big pink daisy in her hair would look awesome in the picture.

Raymond returned with the camera. He and Daisy took several pictures. After seeing the pictures, Blanca decided he would be the official campaign photographer.

Now that they had jobs for Min and Raymond, they just needed a job for DeShaye.

As they were thinking about what DeShaye would be best at, Ms. Lilly sent Amber to tell them it was time to come back for lunch. They would have to think about it more when they got to the cafeteria.

When Daisy and Blanca got to the cafeteria, Blanca counted six posters for Madison already on the walls. Kids were pointing to them and talking about the race.

"We better get some Daisy Power in here!" DeShaye warned as she walked up to them. "Madison is getting a lot of attention with her posters. Everybody comes in here to eat lunch, so are they all going to see Madison Superstar for President."

That gave Blanca an idea. She asked, "DeShaye, can you be in charge of making sure we put all the posters in the best spots?"

DeShaye agreed, "You know it, girl. I already put the ones we hung up this morning by the water fountains."

Daisy smiled. With so many good friends helping her, she just might win. This morning she showed up without any definite plan, but by lunch the chaos had been calmed by her campaign manager.

Daisy passed Blanca two of Abuela's homemade brownies. "You're the best campaign manager in the whole school!" she bragged.

At Madison's table, the girls were talking about how silly Daisy's posters were. They said that Daisy was starting too late to compete with their superstar. Someone even suggested that they pass out candy.

Madison loved the idea and planned to bring some the next day. For Madison, losing was not an option. She didn't believe in losing and she was used to getting her own way, too!

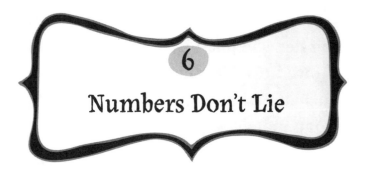

6
Numbers Don't Lie

The next day, Madison did have her candies, but Daisy had candy, too. Her mami had spotted some cute mini daisy lollipops at the dollar store and bought two whole bags of them for Daisy to take to school.

Abuela, Paola, and Daisy tied bright strips of paper on them that said, "Vote for Daisy!" They turned out super cute.

DeShaye and Min were going to stand by the front doors to the school and pass them out. Daisy was waiting for them by the office. As they came in, Min handed Daisy a notebook. Inside were several announcements for the campaign:

Vote for Daisy Power! I have great ideas for student council.

I will listen to all students and be fair. It's the hour for flower power!

Daisy does good things! I'm caring. I care about kids and our community.

Stars are nice, but smarts are better! Vote for me I'm a straight A student.

Don't stop to smell the roses, rush out and vote for flower power!

"Min these are all so awesome I don't know which one to choose first!" Daisy exclaimed. Kids were taking the lollipops, but some of them were also walking over and getting Madison's candy. It was hard to tell if they would be voting for Daisy or Madison.

Blanca arrived just in time to advise Daisy on which announcement would be the best for her first time to speak to the students. She liked the one that said, "Vote for Daisy Power! I have great ideas for student council."

Blanca explained, "It really says everything, because you do have great ideas, Daisy!"

Right before the bell was going to ring, Daisy went to the office. Principal Donaldson led the pledge. Then, he talked about the PTA Family Science Night at the end of the month.

Daisy wished he would hurry up. She was pretty nervous. Finally, he handed her the microphone.

"Hi, my name is Daisy Martinez," she said. She then said her slogan with confidence. It wasn't so bad once she got started.

When she was done, Principal Donaldson patted her on the back and said, "Congratulations, young lady. You did a good job today."

Daisy smiled and thanked him. Then she raced off to her classroom. When she opened the door Madison blurted out, "Ms. Lilly, Daisy is late!"

Their *maestra* said, "Now Madison, you know she was making an announcement. We all heard Daisy talking about her campaign and asking for votes."

Then she said, "Class, we will be visiting the library today to check out books about pilgrims, Jamestown, and Plymouth Rock. Please line up at the door."

One by one, the rows made their way to the door. Blanca, Daisy, and Raymond were at the end of the line. Blanca said, "It's just like *loco* Madison to try to get you in trouble over being late when you weren't really."

Daisy shrugged, "I think she's mad, because I made the first announcement and she didn't think of it." Blanca agreed.

Raymond tapped Daisy on the shoulder. "Daisy, I have some stuff to show you when we get back," he said quietly. She nodded as they all filed into the library.

The librarian gave them some search tips for the computer catalog to locate the books they needed for their research. Daisy loved reading, so she was always in the library checking books out. She knew just what section to look in for books on history. They were in the 900s.

Blanca, Raymond, and Daisy headed right over. Finding the book she needed was easy. She was happy to help her friends, too. When everyone had checked out something to use as a resource, their teacher lined them up to go back to class.

Raymond was very anxious. He pulled Daisy toward the front of the line. He insisted, "You're not going to believe all the stuff I made last night."

Back in room 210, Raymond pulled up two large stacks of sticker printer paper. They had big colorful daisies, but instead of centers they had pictures of Daisy's face in the middle. The petals all had the word *Daisy* on them.

Blanca gasped, "Raymond those are really cute! Did you make them by yourself?"

Raymond turned red and stuttered, "Yeah, it's no problem. I'm good at this computer stuff." He pulled out a fat tube of rolled up paper.

Raymond slowly unwound what Daisy thought was going to be a banner. As the last piece rolled onto the floor she exclaimed, "Wow!" It was the photo he had taken the day before, but he had made it life-sized.

If she stood beside it, people would think it was her twin. It had a bubble by her mouth that said, "Vote for me! Vote for Daisy Power! Vote for someone nice!"

Daisy didn't know what to say. It was really amazing. Finally, Raymond pointed out, "It's for your campaign headquarters. Do you like it?"

Daisy said, "I love it. Thank you, Raymond. I can't wait to put it on the door."

Ms. Lilly came in after the last student entered the classroom. She said, "Okay, my superstar students, let's shift into our math brains. Today, we are going to take a poll and talk about statistics."

Ms. Lilly explained that they would be working in groups. She passed out a playing card to each student. Daisy got the ten of hearts, so she had to work with the ten of spades, clubs, and diamonds.

Once all the students moved to join their group, Ms. Lilly gave more details. Each group would survey a different grade level. The fourth graders would ask the other grade who they planned to vote for in the student council elections.

Daisy and Madison were only allowed to write down data. It would be awkward for them to ask students who they were voting for.

Daisy and her group had the third grade. They went to every classroom. In room one, there were 13 students voting for Daisy and 5 for Madison. Writing those numbers down was exciting for Daisy, but it was just one class.

The group moved on to room two. In that room, 10 kids were voting for Daisy and 6 for Madison. It was thrilling because Daisy was still in the lead.

In every third grade room, Daisy was ahead in the poll. She tried to remind herself that it was just a poll and only the third grade, but back in room 210 the trend continued.

If the election took place today, Daisy would win it! After looking at the statistics Daisy had an amazing 25 percent lead over Madison. She was super excited!

Madison was not super excited. She accused several groups of cheating. Then she demanded to look at their tally sheets.

"Madison, this is just a poll," Ms. Lilly said gently. "I'm sure no one was cheating. Please calm down. Use this information to help you reach voters in the grades where you don't have a lot of support."

Madison seemed to calm down, until Ms. Lilly also encouraged Daisy to use the information. Madison snarled to Lizzie, "I have a plan of my own. I say we stomp on flower power and I know just how to do it!"

7

Dirty Politics

Daisy and her friends were excited about the information they collected for math class. They could tell Daisy was popular in all grade levels. But in some classes Madison was favored by almost as many students, so it could be a close race.

When Daisy arrived at school early the next day, she found something that made her gasp. Her life-sized poster was ruined. Someone had drawn a big black mustache on her picture.

DeShaye came around the corner and said, "What? That is so bad! And I don't mean it in a good way!" She came closer to inspect the mustache. Then she asked, "Is it marker? Did you see anyone hanging around here?"

Daisy just shook her head sadly. It was hard to find her words when such an awful thing had happened to her.

When Blanca saw the door disaster, she was furious. She wailed, "We better go see if Ms. Lilly is in her room yet. We might have to file a report with Principal Donaldson, too!"

Daisy, DeShaye, and Blanca headed to room 210. Their spirits were as low as they could go. Ms. Lilly was standing on a small ladder putting up a new bulletin board. It had a timeline of the early colonists on it.

Blanca didn't even wait for Daisy to say anything, she jumped right in yelling, "Ms. Lilly, you've just got to do something! Someone, and I'm pretty sure Madison knows who, destroyed the poster on Daisy's headquarters. Can you punish her or something?"

Ms. Lilly was so startled, she almost fell off the ladder. "Oh my!" she said, regaining her balance. Then she continued, "Blanca, do you have any evidence? What damage was done?"

Daisy finally spoke up. She described the unfortunate mustache on her picture.

DeShaye added, "I can be mean, but you can actually be too mean. Whoever did this was beyond rude. It is so wrong. I hope when we catch them they get suspended."

This made Ms. Lilly's eyes pop open wide. She exclaimed, "Whoa! Just a minute now girls. You need proof before you can accuse another student."

Blanca never responded when Ms. Lilly asked if they had any evidence, because they didn't have any! Daisy admitted that they did not know who had committed the crime.

Their teacher decided to inspect the poster, so they all went back to the Daisy Power headquarters. Sure enough, the Daisy on the door had a mustache just like Principal Donaldson's.

Ms. Lilly cried, "Oh no! This really is a shame. I can't believe any of our superstar

students would be so unkind. Perhaps we should get the janitor, Mr. Harris, to see if he noticed anything unusual."

Just like that, their teacher turned and sped down the hall toward the office. In the meantime, Min walked up and suggested they change the door decoration.

"We have extra Daisy posters," she said. "Let's use them. My mother always says the best way to defeat an enemy is to make a friend."

Daisy was getting tired before the first bell of the day even rang. Tacking some Flower Power posters on the door she decided, "We're going to let Ms. Lilly handle this. We are only students after all."

When the bell rang, Daisy went to the office to make another announcement for her campaign. The rest of the girls all went to their classes. Madison was waiting outside Principal Donaldson's office with a piece of paper in her hand. She had a smirk on her face.

"You won't be the only one making an announcement today," Madison said. "I have one, too."

Just then Principal Donaldson called them in. After the pledges, he motioned for Daisy to step up to the microphone.

Daisy looked at Madison and said in a clear voice, "Hi, my name is Daisy and I'm running for president of the student council. You know stars are nice, but smarts are better! Vote for me. I'm a straight *A* student."

Then Madison stepped up for her turn. She rambled, "I am the best at everything, so if you want a star for a leader then you better vote for me, Madison Morris."

Daisy had a feeling that if they weren't in the fourth grade, Madison would have finished by sticking her tongue out at her.

All the way back to room 210 neither of them said a word to each other, but as they reached the door Daisy stopped. She said, "Madison, can't we just have a nice, friendly race? I will be happy for you if you're the winner."

Madison stuck her nose in the air and stomped past Daisy to open the door and be the first one inside. Ms. Lilly had other plans, though. When she saw Madison, she asked if she could please see her in the hall for a minute.

Madison spun around. She crashed into Daisy, who bumped into a bookcase with a globe on it. The globe made a small cut on Daisy's arm that bled all over.

Ms. Lilly asked Madison to sit down. Then, she had Daisy come to her desk to get a pass to the nurse. Finally, she buzzed the office so that Mr. Harris could come and clean up the blood on the floor, shelf, and globe.

Shortly after Mr. Harris finished cleaning up, Daisy returned with a large bandage on her arm.

Blanca asked, "Did you break your arm, too?"

Daisy shrugged then replied, "No. The nurse is out today." That explanation seemed to satisfy Blanca.

Raymond poked her in the back. He mumbled, "You okay? If you're really hurt, Madison might win. Maybe that was her evil plan all along."

Daisy frowned and said, "Don't get carried away, Raymond." Even while she was saying it she was thinking about the way Madison ignored her request to keep the race nice.

That night at dinner, Daisy told her family about what happened. Mami said, "Daisy, it's more important to be a good person than to be a president."

Papi reminded her that goodness is often rewarded. He said, "Do you remember when I found a wallet in the parking lot and the store manager said the owner was giving a $100 reward?"

Everyone remembered. They used the money to go the movies. It was a real treat!

Daisy knew her parents were right. No matter what happened tomorrow she would continue to be good. No mean tricks, she promised.

It turned out to be much harder than she expected. In the week before the election, more of Daisy's posters were either torn or mysteriously missing each day. It was a lot of work to keep making replacement posters.

DeShaye and Blanca wanted to take down all Madison's posters and hide them. It was hard to stop them from trying to get back at Madison. She had to keep reminding them that they had no proof of who the poster thief was.

One day, Raymond even tried a stakeout after school. He didn't see a thing. Daisy hoped the mean pranks would stop after the election!

8
Speech! Speech!

The next week, there was a school-wide assembly on Wednesday. All of the candidates for president, vice president, secretary, and treasurer would get to make speeches.

Over the weekend, Mami and Abuela took Daisy shopping for a new navy blue blazer to wear over her jumper. She also got a red daisy for her hair.

Daisy and Min had been working on her speech for five whole days. When Wednesday finally arrived, Daisy woke up tired. She had been too excited to sleep. Before she'd gone to bed, she had practiced her speech by saying it for Abuela, Mami and Papi, and finally for her brothers and sisters.

Abuela cheered, "*¡Bueno trabajo,* Daisy!"

Mami and Papi told her that whether she won or lost they were extremely proud of her. Her brothers booed, but Paola clapped loudly. Carmen cooed.

Daisy knew she was ready, even if her stomach felt like it was full of tiny bouncy balls. She rubbed her damp hand on her jumper before she went downstairs for breakfast.

Abuela made a special breakfast with scrambled eggs, spicy chorizo sausage, and fresh warm tortillas. Yummy!

Mami and Abuela both gave Daisy a big hug and wished her luck before she left for school. When she got to class, she noticed that Madison had on a navy blue blazer, too!

"Oh no, you two look like twins," Blanca said. "Are you going to wear your jacket anyway?"

Daisy was torn. Mami and Abuela were so excited about the special "presidential" coat, but Daisy did not want to be like someone else.

"I have to think about it," she decided. The speeches were scheduled for ten o'clock. At nine thirty Ms. Lilly bragged, "Class, we are very special. We have the only two candidates for student council president. Good luck, superstars!"

Then, Daisy and Madison went to the auditorium to prepare for the assembly. The principal reminded them that the presidential candidates would speak last. After that, he flipped a quarter to see who would go first.

Madison yelled out, "Heads!"

Principal Donaldson moved his hand to show good old George Washington. Madison floated over to her seat, thrilled to be going first.

The more Daisy thought about it, the more she decided it was better to go last. Everyone would remember what you said. It would all be fresh on their minds.

The auditorium began to fill up. Soon the noise level began to go up as well.

Daisy swallowed hard. It was almost time. Madison was tapping her fingers on her knee. She was probably nervous, too. It seemed like the other candidates were taking forever.

One candidate for treasurer had a friend dress up in a gorilla costume and run around on the stage. This caused a *lot* of noise and excitement in the auditorium.

Finally, Principal Donaldson called Madison to the stage. "Students, Madison Morris for president will now give her speech," he announced.

Lizzie and several other girls joined Madison on the stage. They all had red, white, and blue pom-poms. They began to cheer, "Madison, Madison, she's the one. She'll be president when she's done."

Madison adjusted the microphone. She leaned forward and began to say something, but a shrill noise caused kids to cover their ears. The principal motioned for her not to stand so close.

Madison moved back and began again, "Fellow Townsend Elementary students, as you know, I am running for student council president. I will win because I am smarter than anyone at this school. My friends are the coolest kids in fourth grade.

"Every time I look around our school, I see so many things that I can improve. I know most of you would enjoy lunch more if I had the cafeteria painted pink and change the menu so we can have pizza for lunch every day. My plan is to have lip gloss in the girl's restrooms.

"If I win, I will not allow homework on the weekends. We will have dances every month. There will be a special fourth grade area on the playground. No little kids will be allowed!

"We can chew gum or eat candy during class if I win. You know that I am a superstar and would make a super president. Vote for me, Madison Morris."

Then the girls began to cheer again as they ran off the stage. Principal Donaldson looked a little mad. He said, "Now, please welcome Daisy Martinez candidate for student council president."

Daisy did not have gorillas or cheerleaders. But, she did have a great speech that Min helped her write. She did not stand too close and began in a soft voice, "*Hola,* friends and fellow classmates. I am Daisy Martinez. Today I want to tell you about the many reasons that Daisy Power is good for our school.

"First, I will not make promises that I can't keep. I will promise to listen to you, the students. Then I will take your concerns to the student council, teachers, and our principal.

"I plan to request to have student council representatives start a tutoring club to help you with homework one day a week after school.

"I hope to get permission to have a spring dance. We can all make a difference and have fun, too. Daisy Power is all about being good to each other, the school, our community, and our world. If you want a positive president, then vote for me. We are winners! Thank you."

When she was finished, the room burst into applause. Raymond shouted, "Daisy Power!"

Blanca ran up and hugged her as she left the stage. She blurted out, "You were awesome. I just know you're going to win!"

Daisy thought they would find out soon enough. The next day was voting day . . .

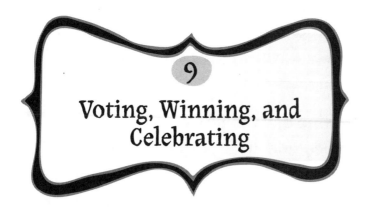

9
Voting, Winning, and Celebrating

That night Paola entertained the whole family by pretending to be a news reporter. She gave all of the details of the presidential speeches.

Daisy did not even mind when her hermana described what she was wearing. As soon as she had gotten home that day, she had told Mami and Abuela all about Madison's jacket. They understood when she explained how important it was for her to be her own person.

Papi gave her a high five. He said, "I really think you have wonderful ideas. You will win, just wait and see!"

Daisy knew she would have another night without much sleep. She thought her mind would not want to shut off. When she finally got in bed, voting was on her mind more than winning.

Voting day was so exciting! You got to make a choice and it could change things. Blanca wanted Daisy at school by six thirty. That way she could be at the front doors to greet students while Blanca, Raymond, DeShaye, and Min passed out the Daisy Power stickers.

When Daisy got to school, she saw that they were voting in the library. It was just like real voting.

Daisy had gone with her parents and Abuela when they voted for the president. They had a screen so no one could see your votes. In the library they had cardboard screens on the tables. Before you went to vote you got a ballot and a pencil to mark it with. When you were done you

put your ballot in the ballot box to be counted. Then you got a sticker saying, "I voted today!"

Daisy hesitated for one second before voting for herself. It seemed kind of wrong to vote for yourself, but DeShaye said, "Girl, if you don't believe in yourself, no one else will." It would be awful if she lost by one vote and didn't vote for herself.

By the end of the day, they would know who won the student council elections. The day was going to creep by. It seemed like a week before it was time for lunch.

There was a lot more noise than usual in the cafeteria. Kids were talking about if they had been to vote yet and who they voted for.

Min had pork pot stickers for lunch. Daisy had pork tamales. DeShaye was eating a school lunch and making fun of Madison's pizza menu.

"Pizza for lunch every day is something not even the principal can do," DeShaye said.

"There are rules about feeding kids healthy foods!"

Min brought up the lip gloss again. She groaned, "Lip gloss in the bathroom is a gross idea. We could all end up with flu."

It seemed the other tables had similar complaints about Madison's plans. Madison seemed unaware. She and her friends were eating vanilla victory cupcakes with red and blue sprinkles.

Every few minutes, her friends would begin to shout, "Madison, Madison, Madison!"

Raymond finally pleaded, "Can't you save it for later? I'm trying to eat."

They ignored him of course.

Back in room 210 the class was working on math again. Daisy had already decided not to get upset if she lost. But she was hoping that her good ideas would help her get the votes she needed to win.

It was nearly three o'clock by the time Principal Donaldson announced the winners. Blanca and Daisy jumped up out of their seats. They were hardly breathing as they waited to hear who would be the next president.

Madison sat perfectly still, acting like she didn't care. But Daisy knew it mattered to Madison.

First, Principal Donaldson declared Jonas Brooks from fourth grade the treasurer. They all clapped, even though no one ran against Jonas. He had to win.

Then, the third grader Grace Lin was announced as secretary. She was very organized and had neat handwriting. She said so in her speech.

Eric Peterson was declared the new vice president. It sounded as if the clock ticking was a train on a track.

Principal Donaldson said, "Congratulations to the new Townsend Elementary student council president, Daisy Martinez. I have to say, I really liked some of your ideas."

Daisy and Blanca were jumping up and down, hugging and screaming. Raymond had his hands over his ears.

Madison looked like she got hit with a baseball. She kept saying, "I don't get it. I'm wonderful. Who didn't vote for me?"

No one was listening. Her classmates were gathered around Daisy to give her a hug or congratulate her. Ms. Lilly was last.

"I'm so proud of our very own presidential superstar!" Ms. Lilly said. "Daisy, you are awesome."

"Ms. Lilly, can I go call my mom and tell her I won?" Daisy asked.

"Absolutely," Ms. Lilly said.

In the office Daisy dialed the number for home. Abuela picked up the phone. Daisy just had to tell Mami first. She asked, "Can I talk to Mami, *por favor*?"

Abuela didn't need to wait to be told. Mami was yelling, "¡Daisy *es la presidenta!*"

Daisy had a lot to celebrate and lot of work ahead of her, but with Daisy Power she could do anything!

Spanish Glossary

abuela – grandmother

amiga – a female friend

¡Bueno trabajo, Daisy! – Good work, Daisy!

Daisy *es la presidenta!* – Daisy is the president!

Daisy *para presidenta* – Daisy for president

hermana – sister

hermano – brother

hola – hello

loco – crazy

maestra – teacher

mi ja – my dear

por favor – please